ONE MORE DRINK

New Year Bae-Solutions

ELLE WRIGHT

Recommended Reading

ONE MORE TRIP TO WELLSPRING...

One More Drink is set in the fictional town of Wellspring, Michigan.

I first introduced Veronica and Juke in my WELLSPRING Series—Touched By You, Enticed By You, & Pleasured By You. For the best reading experience, I encourage you to start with this series before you read One More Drink.

———

Unimaginable luxury. Longstanding wealth. A powerful family empire that controls the town of Wellspring, Michigan. But three heirs are done—with all of it. Now one by one, these very different siblings are seizing control of their lives . . . and daring to find real hometown love.

TOUCHED BY YOU

She's falling hard for the troubled newcomer who saved her life —and holds dangerous secrets.

ENTICED BY YOU

When he is rear-ended by a gorgeous stranger, he finds himself torn between business and pleasure.

PLEASURED BY YOU

He's built a life for himself away from his domineering father and his hometown… but a chance meeting with the woman who has a hold on his heart changes everything.

One More Drink

Everything about my life is different than before. My dead-beat father died, but I found the family of my wildest dreams. I have more money than I ever thought I'd have, yet all I want is one kiss, one shot with him. The only problem? He's the hot bartender I always fantasize about, the confidante who never lectures, and the gentleman who never quite gets the hint.

How many more drinks do I have to order before he sees that I'm not just his friend's newfound sister, but I might be *his* one chance at forever?

Maybe just one more...

Dear Reader

A good (and very wise) friend once told me to "stop *thinking* about everything you want to say and just write the damn story." She was right.

Visiting Wellspring again was just what I needed at this time in my life. I LOVE this town. It was so much fun catching up with some familiar faces.

I fell in love with Veronica and Juke the moment I started writing this story. I went through the gamut of emotions with them. But I enjoyed every bit of it. I hope you do, too.

Love,

Elle

www.ellewright.com

For Granny! I miss you every day!

Chapter One

VERONICA

"*Happy* New Year!"

The chorus of cheers, the sounds of laughter, the echo of happy conversation surrounded me. But my eyes were glued to the man in front of me. He leaned forward, his eyes glued to my lips. I swallowed, waiting for the touch that I'd longed for, the brush of his mouth against mine that I'd dreamed about.

My eyes fluttered closed as his scent wrapped around me. *Shit.* He smelled like he always did, like soap and leather and man. I braced myself for the contact, for the kiss that would, hopefully, segue into something more. Like his hands over my clit, his teeth scraping my nipple, and his dick giving me exactly what I needed tonight. A good fuck with all three "Hs"— *Hot. Heavy. Hard.*

His soft lips met... my forehead? *What the hell is this bull-shit?* I blinked. My eyes popped open and the room slowly

1

returned to focus. The same eyes were staring at me and I was *still* a horny, frustrated woman.

"Happy New Year," Juke whispered, a soft smile on his lips. The lips I had hoped would be kissing me senseless right about now. His mouth brushed my ear. "Happy Birthday, Ronnie."

Nobody called me "Ronnie" except my mom and my… bartender. Because that's exactly who Julian "Juke" Bush was to me now. Not my friend, not my booty call, not my forever love… *just* my bartender.

Yep, I was angry. In fact, I was so pissed I wanted to push him. Not that he would fall over, or even move an inch against the force of my strongest attempt. After all, he was a solid—at least two hundred and twenty pounds—rock of hard muscle with sexy, distracting tattoos, a killer smile, and a seductive voice.

Letting out a frustrated grunt, I deadpanned, "Thanks." *Asshole*.

He frowned. "Are you okay?"

Hell no. "Yes," I bit out through clenched teeth.

"You're sure?" He raised a brow and brushed a strand of hair from my face.

See! It was just that kind of thing that made me want him. Every day, he did something endearing and genuine and sincere.

"Happy Birthday!"

I froze, mortified by what was likely about to happen. "Oh no," I murmured. The loud cheers behind me, nearing me, made me want to run far away from this place, from *his* bar. Brook's Pub was jam-packed with people, as was the tradition in good ol' Wellspring, Michigan. Every year, Juke closed his bar to the public and hosted a private New Year's Eve party. "Please, don't …"

The familiar chorus of Stevie Wonder's version of the

birthday song pierced the air. The crowd was dancing, bumping hips, and singing at the top of their lungs. All for me. *Great.* Too bad I hated my birthday. It came every year, of course, but I'd always been able to avoid celebrating because it was also the holiday.

"Veronica!" my sister, Brooklyn, screamed—right next to my ear. I cringed. "It's your birthday!" she sang, squeezing my shoulders. "Happy Birthday, sis!"

Plugging my ear, I forced a smile on face and turned to face everyone. The damn song went on and on, but when it was finally over, I said, "Thanks." My best lighthearted response paled in comparison to their birthday greetings, but it would have to do.

The candles on the huge cake being held by my younger brother, Bryson, taunted me. It was a lot of them damn things glowing in the dimly lit bar. Once daylight hit, I might be tempted to kill all of them.

Bryson smiled. "It's your day. Go ahead and blow them out."

"She might be too old," Parker announced with a wide grin.

I glared at my oldest brother. "If I'm old, you're old."

He laughed. "Just blow the damn candles out. Kennedi needs a slice of that cake. Stat."

Meeting the gaze of my very pregnant sister-in-love, I said, "Can't disappoint my niece." But instead of blowing the candles out, I quickly removed each one, dropping them into a pitcher of water on the bar top next to me. Everyone cheered. I plastered on that fake smile again. "Thanks, everyone. I appreciate you." I hugged my siblings. "I need a drink."

Still frustrated, I turned and nearly bumped into Juke, who hadn't moved from his spot. Sighing, I shoved him aside and limped over to the bar.

I slid onto a barstool and kicked off my shoes, cussing out those high ass heels under my breath. I'd purchased them with this occasion in mind. Hell, I'd worn my sluttiest dress and even paid a makeup artist to give me a smoky eye. Because I was on a mission—*Operation Fuck Me, Juke.* Normally, I'd be at home in my pajamas watching the ball drop with a bottle of sparkling apple cider.

Moving to Wellspring a couple of years ago had also brought on a change in my holiday traditions. A few burgers on the grill on Memorial Day had morphed into a full barbecue dinner with ribs so tender I wanted to weep *and* outdoor games. My Thanksgiving was nothing like the quiet dinners I used to have with my mother and stepfather. It was a weekend affair starting with the Wellspring Thanksgiving Parade and ending with a competitive bowling tournament. And Christmas... Breakfast in the morning, lunch, and a six-course dinner. Oh, and lots of gifts.

I should be feeling happy, grateful even. But this day had never been *my* day.

"Veronica?" Brooklyn joined me, sliding onto the stool next to mine. "What's going on?"

"Nothing," I lied.

"Yeah, right. If you're going to lie, at least try to make it convincing. Your whole face betrays you."

I blew out a harsh breath and ordered shot of Patrón because champagne wasn't going to cut it. "I'll be fine, Brooklyn."

Not because I really *was* okay, but because I always *had* to be good. No matter what was going on in my life, I was expected to grin and bear it. Even through hurt feelings, tears, and life's disappointments, my mother had always ordered me to suck it up and trust God. Broken bones? Thank God you have a doctor. Liver and onions? Be

4

grateful you have food on the table. Boyfriend dumped me? Praise the Lord. He wasn't the man for you. God was looking out. Cry? So many people have it worse. Depressed? No faith. Jesus would work it out.

At six, I'd had to sit out the Daddy-Daughter dance because my father didn't want me. I'd never received anything from him. Not a call, a card, a gift. I would have settled for a letter in a plain white envelope and a thirty cent stamp. I never complained, though. The fact that he couldn't be bothered to even call me on my birthday because I was a girl and not an heir to the Wellspring Water Corporation still stung. But I'd needed that call, I'd yearned to be acknowledged by him. I hated that feeling of not being wanted. *I still hate it.*

"Sis?" Brooklyn rubbed my back. "You can talk to me. Tell me what's wrong? I want to help you."

I shot my sister a sidelong glance. "I know you do, but I don't think you can."

She frowned. "Even if I can't, I can still listen."

My eyes watered but I willed the tears not to fall. It was New Year's Day, damn it. No emotions, no tears, no heart-to-hearts in the middle of Brook's Pub. "Maybe another time," I said, offering her a small smile. I downed the shot in front of me and relished in the burn traveling down my throat and settling in my gut.

"Fine." Brooklyn ordered two more shots. "If you want to drink, I'll drink with you. Carter can drive us both home."

I smirked. "I'm sure he would love that, handling *two* drunk women tonight?"

Shrugging, Brooklyn said, "If he doesn't, oh well. I'll still suck his dick tonight, so he'll be just fine."

Unable to help myself, I laughed. Loudly. And it felt good. "Thank you for that, sis."

"You know I got you." The bartender, *not Juke*, set two full shot glasses on the bar in front of us. I picked up one and Brooklyn grabbed the other. "Toast?"

"To what?" I eyed her skeptically. "Please don't say another year. That's so cliché."

"Girl! What the hell is going on with you? Birthdays are national holidays. I've been trying to tell you this forever."

"Not forever," I countered. "I literally just met you a few years ago."

Brooklyn giggled. "Oh, shut up. One day, you'll tell me why you hate your birthday so much."

"Let me guess… this," I motioned toward the cake that had been cut and served already, "was your idea."

"It was," Brooklyn admitted. "And I know you told us not to make a big deal, but I wanted to. I didn't get a chance to steal your birthday thunder while we were kids. And since I've grown out of that center of attention phase, I had to do something special for you. To thank you for being my sister. To celebrate you because you're a bad ass boss. Smart as hell. Beautiful. Kind. Fly in every way. You deserve birthday cake." She met my watery gaze. "If Kennedi doesn't eat it all," she added under her breath.

Before my father died, I'd spent a lot of years feeling alone, like I didn't have a place in the world. Parker Wells Sr. had effectively prevented me from bonding with brothers who would have protected me against every enemy, real or imagined. My bastard of a father kept me from hours of advice and support from my sister. And now that he was gone, I'd stepped into a world I had only dreamed of in what seemed like a past life. Family. Friends. Everything I didn't know I wanted, but so desperately needed.

"I hate my birthday," I confessed softly. "It has never felt like *my* day."

"Why?"

I hunched my shoulders. "Growing up, we prayed for the New Year and spent the day at church."

"That sucks," Brooklyn grumbled. "No birthday parties?"

"Not really. My mom didn't celebrate birthdays. She thought it was a waste of money to eat empty calories and blow your spit onto cake that other people would eat. It just wasn't a priority for her."

While she'd spent years being Senior's mistress, my mother had been determined to leave her past behind. After I was born, Susan Pittman became Reverend Pittman. She'd turned her life over to God and had never looked back.

I sighed. "I love my mother, but she was definitely about that church life."

Brooklyn nodded. "And so you had to be, too?"

"Pretty much," I admitted. "I didn't hate it, though. I learned a lot from her. She gave me a good life."

"Your mother is good people. She's always been nice to me. Probably because she doesn't really know about my penchant for foul language. I'm certain she wouldn't approve of our cussing and drinking ways."

"My mother would probably send me to the altar over the amount of alcohol I've imbibed since I moved here."

We laughed until tears of mirth fell. "Drinks are good for the soul. However, I'm sure that comment won't age well when we wake up in the morning."

"That part." I held up my glass. "Well, to hangovers and blow jobs."

"Now, that's a muthafuckin' toast!"

We took our shots, no chaser. "Woo." I blew out a harsh breath. "That was good."

"Hell yeah, it was. Now," she turned to face me, "what is up with you and Juke?"

With narrowed eyes, I said, "Did you give me tequila to learn all of my secrets?"

"No, but you two looked super cozy when the clock struck midnight. Did you finally get your kiss?"

I snorted. "No."

Frowning, Brooklyn ordered two more shots—one more than I should've had. "What? You look hot. He should have been kissing your ass all over this bar."

"Except he didn't. All I got for my trouble was a fore-head kiss."

Brooklyn choked on the water she'd drank. "What the hell was he thinking? This isn't *The Best Man*. Forehead kisses are not what's up."

"Right? Especially since I am dressed to get some. It's like he can't catch a hint. I don't know what I'm doing wrong. I keep trying to switch to the fast lane of friends who fuck. And he's firmly stuck in the slow lane of friends who… just friend."

Brooklyn cracked up, dropping her head on the bar. "You're hilarious."

"It's not funny."

Yet, the joke always seemed to be on me. I wouldn't consider myself the best flirt, but I thought I was throwing out good hints. Juke and I talked every single day, whether on the phone, via text, or in person. We had dinner at least once a week. Shit, I even joined the bowling league so I could show him I was good with balls. And tonight? My dress was a whole sexy vibe, my skin was glowing and *showing*. Full cleavage on display.

8

"I mean, what do I have to do? Throw myself on his dick?"

Brooklyn's smile fell. "Uh oh."

"He's behind me, isn't he?"

She nodded.

Damn.

I let out a heavy, embarrassed sigh and turned to face him. "Hi," I croaked. "So, you heard me."

Juke's gaze dropped to my mouth. "I did."

Steeling myself, I went with bad ass bravado. "Good. I meant that shit."

Then, I walked away.

Chapter Two

LONG ISLAND NO TEA

JUKE

"Wish in one hand, shit in the other. See which one fills up first."

A long time ago, my granny told me that shit. I'd just received the bad news that I'd gotten cut from the freshman football team because I was too slow. It was just one of many sayings she'd toss into the air as if it made perfect sense. Except, it didn't make sense to me then because my world consisted of food, school, and sports. At the time, I thought she'd been sneaking sips of the gin she'd kept in her bedside drawer.

Once I'd figured it out, though, my life changed. I could either spend all day wishing I'd made the team or I could work my ass off to make it a reality. I chose to run every morning until I increased my speed. I threw away the junk food and lost twenty pounds. I cut grass and raked leaves so that I could pay for a personal trainer. And I attended every football game and studied the plays. The next year, I made the team.

Since then, I'd built my life with my granny's words playing on repeat in my head. I considered myself successful—money in the bank, investments, property, good health. My bar was a focal point in my town, the hottest bar in area. Tourists and Wellspringers had put Brook's Pub on the map. Not bad for a small town man who'd lost both parents before turning eight. I would continue to do my thing, too. Because whenever I wanted something? I worked for it, I planned for it, I pursued it.

So… What the hell was I thinking?

Ronnie had arrived at the bar, stunning in every way. I couldn't take my eyes off of her. I hadn't even bothered to hide my perusal. Not when she'd winked at me as she strolled toward her siblings. Not when she'd tipped her head at me after I'd personally delivered her a glass of champagne. Not when she'd turned every single mutha-fucka away who'd tried to holla. And definitely not when she'd blessed me with a knowing smile when the DJ played her favorite song, which also happened to be *my* favorite, "You Gots To Chill" by EPMD.

The party was lit, but I didn't give a fuck. Wellspring was home. The people here? Family. Yet, the only thing, the only person I wanted to be with tonight was *her*. I knew what I wanted. I'd known for a long time. Tonight, an opportunity had presented itself. Despite the amount of people there, the countless questions from my staff, and the many requests from other guests, I'd managed to end up right next to Ronnie just before the countdown started. I was ready, aimed, and I fuckin' misfired. How the hell did my lips connect with her forehead and not her full mouth? *Shit.*

"Um, sir!"

Ouch. "Damn, Brooklyn." I rubbed my forehead where she'd thumped the hell out of me. "What the hell was that for?" And why didn't I notice she was still beside me and not on the other side of the bar with her husband and siblings?

Brooklyn rolled her eyes and waved a dismissive hand in my face. "You're not this stupid, Juke. But you *are* a punk."

I blinked. "What?"

"Veronica!" Brooklyn raised her hands, mimicking a choke-hold. "I would shake your ass if I had the strength to make a difference. Or to make you fall."

I couldn't help but smile. Because no matter what was going on in my life, Brooklyn could always make me laugh. It'd been that way since we were in elementary school.

"Seriously, Juke." Brooklyn finished her glass of water. "My sister is hot as hell."

Ronnie was always beautiful, but tonight, she looked almost ethereal. Too perfect for this town or even this world. Definitely, for me. That tight ass dress, those legs, the hint of skin that begged me to reach out and touch her, made me want to drop to my knees and surrender. And that had been the plan. Until I'd choked. Now, she was gone and I was standing there watching her bless these other niggas with her smile.

"Don't you think I know that?" I grumbled.

"You heard her. She wants you."

I thought about Ronnie's confession to Brooklyn. I'd definitely be down for anything that involved her throwing herself on my dick. But it was more than that.

There was something about Veronica Wells. From the moment she'd entered my bar with Bryson, I was intrigued. Because, damn, she was fine as hell. But she was also smart and funny and sweet. We'd bonded over music, more specifically hip-hop. The commonalities didn't end with EPMD or Eric B. & Rakim either. Right there at her favorite barstool, we'd talked about our childhoods, politics, sports, and food. And every time I heard a *Ronnie Story*, I wanted to know more. Soon, I started looking forward to her visits—her smile, her scent… *That ass.*

"The girl was waiting for you to make your move," Brooklyn continued, "and you choked with a damn forehead kiss and a dopey smile. Ugh!" She thumped me again.

That shit hurt.

"Like you were her uncle or something," she added. "No, like you were her brother. What's the problem?"

"I don't have a problem." I lied. There *was* a problem, one that I didn't necessarily want to talk about tonight. Not yet.

Brooklyn arched a brow and pressed her pointed nail against my nose. "Bullshit."

"Cut that shit out," I grumbled, pushing her hand away from my face.

"Tell me I'm wrong."

I never could lie to her. "You're not."

Folding her arms across her chest, Brooklyn said, "Okay, then. What happened?"

Sighing, I pulled Brooklyn toward my private booth. Because we had to be alone for this conversation. The last thing I wanted was to be fodder for Wellspring's morning gossip.

"Sit," I ordered.

She did as I asked. Leaning forward, she whispered, "You're impotent."

I laughed. "What?"

Placing her hand over mine, she gave me her famous somber social worker, *I'm-here-for-you* gaze. "It's okay to say

ELLE WRIGHT

it out loud. If you can't perform, they have meds for that now." She giggled, squeezing my hand. "I'm just kidding. What's up?"

I shook my head. "You're crazy as hell."

"I'm so drunk right now," she admitted. "This is what happens when the baby spends the night with Grandma. Drinks and lots of sex! Ha!" She clapped, cracking up at herself. "I'll be back to normal tomorrow."

Once again, I couldn't help but laugh at her antics. I arched a brow. "If you're not *Normal Brooklyn*, why am I talking to you right now?"

Her smile fell. "Good point." Clearing her throat, she straightened in her seat. "Okay, I'll pull myself together for this conversation. Go ahead."

I waved a server over and asked her to bring a pitcher of water and food to sober my friend up.

"I just knew you were going to give us a show," Brooklyn said.

"I wanted to."

"For a long time."

"Yeah."

Brooklyn grinned. "I'm glad you're finally admitting it."

Shrugging, I told her, "It is what it is." Seconds later, the server arrived with water and a plate of hummus, whole-wheat pita chips, and veggies. *The Drunk Special.* I pushed the plate toward Brooklyn. "Eat this."

She dipped a piece of celery into the hummus and tasted it. Once she finished the stalk, she sat back. "I still don't see the problem. Veronica was there, waiting for you. And you let her down. You let *me* down."

"And so was Laura." I'd wanted to believe that I didn't let Ronnie's lips slip away because my *friend* just happened to enter the bar right when the clock struck midnight. But I

14

couldn't deny it'd played a role in the last minute decision to not kiss Ronnie the way I'd *planned* to tonight.

Brooklyn glanced around the bar, presumably trying to find Laura in the crowd. Laura had disappeared up the stairs, heading to her apartment that I held vacant for her even though she rarely stayed in town longer than a month at a time. Basically, she used my shit as a luxury storage unit. And I let her.

"She's upstairs," I murmured.

"Whatever. But what does Laura have to do with Ronnie? She's not your woman. And why do you let her come up in here and ruin shit all the time? It's been that way since we were young."

My off-and-on relationship with Laura exhausted the hell out of me on a daily basis. I spent a lot of time *and* money taking care of her. At one point, I thought we'd be more than friends, but she was as selfish as I was loyal.

Still, I'd made sure she always had a place to stay or a spot in my bed when she wanted it. And, tonight, after disappearing for months, she'd walked into my damn bar like she owned it.

"I get it. Believe me." I shifted in my seat. "But she *is* something to me. Which is why I have to nip that shit in the bud before I even bring Ronnie into my life like that."

"Yeah. She's at least three somethings." Brooklyn held up three fingers. "A freeloading bitch, a nasty bitch, and a stupid bitch. I'm sure I can think of more, but you already know she ain't shit. And you know I have no problem saying it to her face. I don't give a fuck."

I barked out a laugh. "Tell me how you really feel."

"No doubt."

My shoulders fell. "When I saw her come in, I couldn't kiss Ronnie. I need to close that chapter before I make a move. Ronnie deserves that much."

Brooklyn let out a string of curses. "Fine. I guess I understand. I just can't stand Laura's crusty ass. Yep, she's a crusty bitch."

I knew Brooklyn's change of heart about Laura had everything to do with me. Years ago, it seemed inevitable that we'd end up together. Years of the back and forth between us, the *will-they-won't-they* shit, had taken its toll on me, though. And Brooklyn had been there more than anyone else to witness the fallout.

"You've been good to that trifling bitch." Brooklyn shook her head in disgust. "You've always deserved better. I just wish you'd realize that."

"I know, Brooklyn. She won't be here long." She never was. But Laura would soon find out what it meant to not have me to fall back on anymore. "Once she sees the notice I left in her room, she'll know it, too."

As if on cue, Laura barreled down the stairs and headed straight for us. "Juke!" She held up a piece of paper and shook it. "What the hell is this?"

"An eviction notice," I told her, keeping my eyes on Brooklyn.

Laura sighed heavily. "Really? You're really doing this to me?"

I folded my arms over my chest and peered up at her. "I think it's time, don't you?"

"No!" She smacked the paper down on the table. "This is bullshit."

"Why not?"

"Because I need you," Laura whined.

Maybe a few months ago, tears in her eyes would have affected me but now... *I got nothing.* "You always need something. Money, a place to stay, an orgasm, a job. But I don't have any of that for you anymore."

"Brooklyn?" Laura glared at my friend. "Can you leave us alone?"

I shook my head when Brooklyn shot me a questioning glance. "She's fine right here," I said. "You're the one that's leaving. Pack your shit. The room will be cleaned out tomorrow and the locks will be changed."

"I have nowhere else to go," Laura cried. "You can't do this to me. What about everything we've been through?" She grabbed my hand. "I came back because I wanted to give us a try."

"Oh, please," Brooklyn muttered.

Laura rolled her eyes at Brooklyn, before she met my waiting gaze again. "Juke, I was scared of us. You've always been so intense. But, baby, there's no one else for me. You have to believe me. You're the man I want."

I snickered, pulling my hand from her grasp. "I'm sure I am, now that you have to find a place to stay."

The mask slipped then. No more tears, no more pleading. The concern in Laura's eyes… gone. "Dammit." She let out a harsh breath. "Well, can I borrow a—"

"No."

"After everything I've done for you?" she snapped.

"What exactly have you done for *me*, Laura?" I asked. "Besides eat my food, drink my liquor, sleep in my apartment, and take my kindness for a weakness."

Laura shook her head. "No. You know we're more than that."

"Only when you need something." I raised a challenging brow. "Right?"

"Forget this. I'm outta here," she hissed.

"Bye," Brooklyn said. "Damn."

"Brooklyn," I warned, pointing at the plate of food. "Eat."

"You're going to regret this, Juke," Laura shouted, drawing the attention of several guests. She picked up the eviction notice, ripped it, and tossed it in my face. "Fuck you! Fuck this damn small-ass town! I hate it here anyway."

Shit. Out of the corner of my eye, I saw several people moving closer to the booth.

Brooklyn stood. "Wait a minute. I know you not—"

I gripped her arm tightly, meeting her furious gaze and pleading with her silently not to cause an even bigger scene than the one developing.

"Fine." Brooklyn clamped her mouth shut and plopped back down into the seat. "I'll just sit my ass down and eat this hummus." She picked up a carrot and bit down on it hard.

I mouthed a quick thank you to her before turning my attention back to Laura. "We're not doing this. It's over. Take your shit and leave."

Laura turned on her heel and stormed back up the stairs, hurling insults at random people the entire way and tossing glassware on the ground. *So much for no scene, no gossip.*

"She's a messy bitch, too," Brooklyn said.

I glared at her. "Don't start."

Blowing out a frustrated breath, she ate a pita chip. "Eating hummus."

Sighing, I stood and announced to the crowd, "Nothing to see here. Drink, eat, and leave it the hell alone." I smiled at Brooklyn. "I'll send Carter over here."

Brooklyn smiled. "Please do. And, Juke?"

"Yes?"

"You did the right thing."

"I know that." I leaned over and kissed her brow. "Thanks for always being there."

"That's exactly how brotherly a forehead kiss should be."

Laughing, I headed toward the bar. On the way, I stopped to pick up a broken glass and tossed it into a nearby trashcan. The party was back in full swing, the music was loud, and everyone seemed sufficiently uninterested in me and my drama. Until tomorrow when I'd hear about how Laura bashed me in the head with a glass before she told me I wasn't shit and walked out, leaving me devastated. The joys of living in a small town. People couldn't wait to tell the story, but it was never right and always outrageous by the time it spread around to everyone who cared to know.

When I glanced around, I noticed Ronnie standing near the pool tables, looking my way. Now that I'd taken care of my Laura problem, there was nothing holding me back. I wanted to go to her, talk to her, finish what I'd hoped to start earlier. But when she turned her back on me and started talking to Bryson and Jordan, I decided to wait.

Something else my granny used to say? "*A delay is not a denial.*" She was right. Tomorrow was another day, another chance to redeem myself. And I was definitely going to take it.

Chapter Three

VERONICA

"*M*ake it stop!" I squeezed my knee, flinching as my friend Stacyee finished the last French braid in my hair. "I think you might have braided my scalp."

Stacyee laughed, swatting my shoulder. "Girl, stop being a baby. I don't even braid tight."

Someone should have reminded me that braids and a hangover didn't mix well. "I should have just put my hair in a ponytail and called it a day," I grumbled, standing and stretching as soon as Stacyee was done. "Or maybe I should cut my hair short like Brooklyn."

"Please, don't." Brooklyn set down her magazine. "My poor sister would be rocking hats until it grew out."

Stacyee gave Brooklyn a high-five. "Right?" She glanced at me. "No offense, but you have no hair skills. It's best for you to keep your hair long."

20

"Shut up," I mumbled, walking over to the mirror to check out the style Stacyee had given me. *Nice. Easy. Me.* They weren't wrong. I'd never been able to do my hair. In college, I had a matching baseball cap for every outfit. And when I didn't wear a hat, I donned my famous ponytail or braids. "Thanks, Stacyee. I appreciate you doing this."

Stacyee stuffed her hair products back in her bag. "I don't know why you wanted braids. I just spent an hour and a half on your hair yesterday. And it looked damn good."

Bryson's wife, Jordan, stepped into the room. "Y'all done? Dinner is almost ready."

The word "room" seemed so small for the space we were currently hiding out in while the men watched football and the kids screamed for no apparent reason. It was more like a luxury she shed, a secret haven complete with a small kitchen, a full bathroom, a bedroom, a sitting area, and a flat screen television.

New Year's dinner was at Jordan and Bryson's home this year, which used to be our father's home. Senior had willed it to my brother, with the caveat that he live in it for one year. Of course, that hadn't gone over well with Bryson due to the abuse he'd experienced in this very home. If Jordan hadn't wound up getting pregnant with my beautiful nieces, Bryson would have probably walked away from it all. And I wouldn't have blamed him. From all accounts, Senior was a monster. I often considered myself lucky to have never experienced the evil side of him. Actually, I'd never experienced *any* side of him. Which, apparently was a good thing.

I nodded. "Yep. All done."

"No!" Stacyee said. "I'm trying to figure out why Veronica wanted me to braid over my masterpiece."

I shrugged. "The party is over."

"But it's still your birthday," Stacyee argued. "That's a big deal."

"Not really." I put my earrings back on. "Besides, I have to drive to Indianapolis in the morning. I'd like to not have to worry about my hair while I'm down there."

My mother had requested my presence at her anniversary dinner. It had been four years since she'd married Pastor Griffin and became Reverend First Lady of Abundant Faith Ministries. The occasion was a huge one for the church and sure to be an all-day event.

"How long will you be gone?" Jordan asked.

"A week." Or two days. Or a day, depending on what happened while I was down there. Not that I didn't enjoy spending time with my mother. It was just… well, there was only so much lecturing I could stomach, only so many questions about my decision to leave my teaching career behind and move to Wellspring. The curiosity surrounding the break-up with my ex was still a topic of conversation in my mother's home, too. Even though, it'd been years and he was now married with a kid on the way. I just didn't want to have to go over the reasons again. They never seemed to be good enough.

More than likely, I'd have to hear all about how my childhood best friend, Miranda, had found her perfect mate, married, and was now a perfect mother of three. Or I'd be subjected to the scriptures on fornication and drinking to excess. And maybe even a little bit of allowing my spiritual gifts to "make room" for me.

"You should have come to the party, Stacyee." Jordan sat on the window seat.

Brooklyn kicked her feet up on an ottoman. "Right. It was quite the event."

I sighed. "It was okay."

"I heard Laura's ass showed up and threw her drink in Juke's face," Stacyee said.

"Girl!" Brooklyn rolled her eyes. "That is not what happened. Not even close."

Jordan shook her head. "People stay making up shit."

Stacyee glanced at me, then at Brooklyn, then at Jordan, then back at me. "So…? What the hell happened?"

"He kicked her ass out finally." Brooklyn finished her bottle of water. "She had a mini-fit and broke some glasses. That's it."

I thought about the scene at the bar. I knew all the gossip surrounding Juke and Laura, because people liked to talk. Part of me had always wanted to ask him about her, but I never had. And he'd never offered. So I'd left it alone. But after the party, I couldn't stop wondering who she really was to him.

Jordan giggled. "I was cracking up when Bryson had to help her off the floor when she tripped up the stairs."

"Damn, I missed that," Brooklyn said.

I hadn't missed it. And I'd laughed as hard as Jordan. In fact, all of us had laughed at Laura's expense for a good ten minutes.

Stacyee grinned. "I wonder if someone caught the footage on their phone. I want to laugh, too."

We all burst out laughing until tears rolled down my face. "What's her deal anyway?" I asked, wiping my cheeks with a tissue.

"She used to be cool," Brooklyn said. "But she changed after she landed a few acting gigs."

I had heard Laura was an actress, but I'd never seen her in anything. "What did she play in?" I asked.

Stacyee frowned. "Play in? Chile, that girl was an extra in a scary movie a few years ago."

"And she died in the first five minutes." Jordan chuckled. "The killer beheaded her. I don't even think she had a speaking part."

"She didn't," Stacyee said. "But you'd think she was the star the way she flounced her ass around here like she was Jada Pinkett-Smith."

"She can't act worth a dime," Brooklyn added. "Trying to get Juke to feel sorry for her. She couldn't even stay in character last night. Switched from broken-hearted to psycho bitch in two-point-two seconds."

Jordan slid on the floor. "I'm dead."

"Seriously," Brooklyn continued, "if Juke hadn't stopped me, I would have gladly kicked her ass."

"Your ass was too drunk to kick anything last night," I said. "Carter had to carry you out of there."

"Damn, I missed Brooklyn getting drunk, too?" Stacyee asked.

"She was outta there," Jordan said.

"Listen!" Brooklyn clapped her hands together. "I would've been sober enough to smack the shit out of her ass."

We talked a few more minutes about Laura and the rest of the party. I thought I was home free until Stacyee asked, "Veronica, did you at least get your midnight kiss?"

"She got a kiss alright," Brooklyn murmured. When I glared at her, she shrugged. "What?"

"No comment." I stood. "Let's go eat."

Without another word, I made my way to the massive dining room. Scanning the area, I marveled at my family.

To my right, Jordan's grandparents were setting up the dessert table. Kennedi's Aunt Anny was adjusting the table settings. On the far end of the room, Parker and Carter were on kid duty. Kennedi strolled into the room holding a punch bowl and Bryson was right behind her with bottles of wine.

"Oops." Brooklyn picked up the box of flatware sitting on the table. "I guess we should have been here sooner."

"I better help bring the food out." Jordan rushed into the kitchen.

Stacyee moved toward the table. "And I'll just sit and get ready to eat."

"Veronica?" Bryson motioned to the table. "Sit. It's still your birthday."

"I can help," I told him.

"Not today." He winked and poured wine into a glass. "We got this."

In that moment, emotion threatened to spill over as tears filled my eyes.

Before my father died, I could count my family on one hand. Now, I had brothers, sisters, sisters-in-love, a brother-in-love, nieces, nephews, and a host of friends who were more like family. The people around me didn't judge me or make their problems my problems. They just loved me.

"Are you okay?"

I jumped, turning to find Juke standing next to me, a smile in his eyes. My gaze dropped to his lips. "Hi," I breathed. "I'm okay. Just thinking about how different my life is."

He searched my eyes. "I hope that's a good thing."

"It is." I gave him my best *I'm-not-really-crying* smile. "I almost have everything I've ever wanted. And I feel extremely blessed."

One tear spilled from my eyes. *Dammit, I'm crying.*

He brushed the tear from my cheek and ran his thumb over my chin. "I get it. Sometimes it's overwhelming. All of this family, all of this love."

I tilted my head and studied him. His Granny had passed away several years ago. I knew from our many conversations that he didn't have much family, other than a few cousins scattered across the country and a brother he didn't talk to at all. Just like me.

"Overwhelming in a good way?" I asked.

Nodding, he agreed. "Exactly."

The concern in his gaze quickly morphed into something else. Heat. And I felt it all over me, from the crown of my sore head to the tips of my toes. Slowly, I exhaled to center myself, to prevent any unfortunate mishaps, like me trying to kiss him again and him… planting another forehead kiss on me.

With his eyes on mine, hypnotizing me with their intensity, he leaned forward. "Ronnie, can we talk?"

"Alone?" I blurted out loudly. I glanced around the room to see if anyone had caught that. When I noticed that no one was even paying attention to us, I turned back to him. "I mean… now?"

"Ronnie?" His voice was a low rumble, a soft plea that pierced my heart.

And my heart wasn't the only thing affected by him. My body was buzzing with desire and need, something I hadn't felt in… ever.

"Please?" he whispered.

That last word did me in. Because I wanted to go with him. I *would* go with him anywhere. Even though I still was low-key irritated with him for that non-kiss, even though I knew we probably needed to have a conversation about it, even though I wanted to know more about Laura and that entire scene at the bar.

"I—"

The clang of silverware against a glass drew my attention away from Juke and toward the center of the room, where Bryson stood at the head of the table. He announced dinner and, soon, everyone took their seats. I glanced back at Juke and shrugged before I rounded the table to my chair.

Dinner lasted longer than I thought it would because the entire time I was focused on Juke. While Grandpa Will said grace, my mind was stuck on Juke instead of the Lord. During the first course, I'd caught him staring at me as he poured gravy on his mashed potatoes. The fried chicken was slappin', but I couldn't concentrate on the goodness of my crispy, perfectly-seasoned wing because I couldn't take my eyes off of him.

Now, with pies being passed, cakes being sliced, and coffee being poured, I had no appetite for sweets. I just wanted to be alone with him.

"Juke brought his famous winter cider," Brooklyn announced as she carried out a pot from the kitchen. "It will go nicely with that pound cake Anny made."

Anny glanced at Juke. "Thanks for bringing it, Juke. I love your warm cider." The older woman grinned. "I heard you got knocked upside the head with a bottle last night."

Kennedi choked. Patting her chest hard, she said, "Anny, where did you get that from?"

Grandma Dee chimed in. "Wait a minute, someone told me Laura threw a plate of vegetables at you and splashed a pitcher of water in your face."

The room erupted in laughter. And I joined them, cracking up when Grandpa Will admitted that he'd heard Laura had slapped Juke's hat off his head before she tipped over a table and tossed a bunch of napkins in the air.

Everyone was laughing now, even Juke.

Finally, Juke said, "I didn't even have on a hat. There were no slaps, no hitting upside the head, and no drinks in my face."

Anny waved him off. "Oh, baby. You know how people like to talk. We're not worried about no Laura." She took a sip of her drink. "'Bout time you kicked that trifling heffa out."

"I'm glad you said it, Ann," Grandma Dee agreed. "I never did like that girl. She always seemed fake."

Laughter filled the room again, then the conversation shifted to other stuff. After a while, Juke poured two glasses of cider, then he stood and motioned with his head for me to follow him.

There were so many rooms in Bryson and Jordan's house, but the sunroom was my favorite. When we entered the quiet space, I made a beeline for the sofa in front of the fireplace, my spot.

Before I bought my condo, I'd spent a lot of time here and enjoyed the sanctuary they'd created. With stunning views of the Grand River, I loved to just sit and watch the beauty that was Wellspring. In the summer, I'd open all the windows and let the breeze flow through the room. In the winter, I'd turn on the fireplace and curl up with a book and a soft blanket. It was my little slice of Heaven on Earth.

I'd always considered myself to be a city person. Actually, I hated the idea of small town living—until I met my siblings, until I visited this town. Now, I couldn't imagine calling anywhere else home. The scenery and the community were a bonus, but the peace I'd always felt here had made my decision easy.

Seconds later, Juke handed me a glass of the warm cider. "What's on your mind?" He sat down next to me, shifting to face me. "Are you okay? You seem sad."

I shook my head. "I'm fine. Just thinking about everything." Staring at the fire, I continued, "Sometimes I wonder how my life would have been different if I'd spent summers here, if I'd been able to come to one

Memorial Day party or Juneteenth celebration. I think about what Christmas would have been like with my brothers and sister. Then, I think about how lonely I was at home."

In that moment, I was acutely aware of him. He didn't speak, but I felt his eyes on me, his scent surrounding me, the heat of his body against mine.

"I've heard all the stories about Senior." I turned to him. "Everyone tells me I'm better off. But I can't help but think it might have been worth the dance with the devil to have the joy of family, of siblings that I could've argued with or competed against or confided in." Shrugging, I added, "Even if it was only once a year."

"For what it's worth," he said, "I was here with them. I've seen more than I ever wanted to. And trust me, you *were* better off. It wasn't pretty."

"I know. My heart breaks for Bryson sometimes because I still see him struggle with things that Senior did to him. I ache for Parker when someone compares his business acumen to our father. And I cry for Brooklyn when she's torn between mourning him and hating him for everything he's done."

"Maybe that's it, then," he suggested. "Maybe what you're feeling is empathy or simply wanting to take the pain away from them. Or maybe it's that protective instinct that I have."

"I definitely feel that."

"That's normal. When my granny was alive, I wanted to protect her from the cancer. I wanted to take the treatments for her. It's hard to see someone you love hurting."

I reached out and rubbed his cheek. "It is."

Closing his eyes, he leaned into my hand. "Thanks," he whispered. "Can I ask you a question?"

The conversation had taken a heavy turn and I wasn't

sure what he'd ask me. But I nodded anyway. "As long as I can I ask you a question."

He chuckled. "Got it. Why do you hate your birthday?"

"I don't hate it. I just…" I sighed. "Okay, I hate it." I let out a humorless laugh. "It never feels like *mine*. Nothing has ever felt like it belongs to only me. Growing up I didn't celebrate because my mom didn't believe in extravagant parties when other people were struggling to make ends meet. Even as an adult, it was all about everyone else's resolutions or their families. And all I wanted was for someone to tell me I was their moon and their stars, that I mattered. I guess my birthday is just a reminder that I didn't feel that growing up."

"You definitely matter, Ronnie," he whispered. "To them and *to me.*"

My heartbeat pounded loud in my ears as his words filled me with hope. "I believe that. I do. Honestly. Being here is everything. I love Wellspring. I'm sure I'll get over the whole birthday melancholy one day. Next year, hopefully. Maybe I'll even make a wish the next time someone buys me a cake."

"Pretend I'm holding your cake, then." He held up his hands, like he had something in them.

I eyed him skeptically. "What?"

"We're thinking happy thoughts right now. Keep up."

I sat up straight. "Okay, I'm good with that."

"If you could have that moment again, what would you wish for?"

Peering up at the ceiling, I bit down on my bottom lip. So many things flashed through my mind. Beaches, mountain cabins, a new career, being in love, a family of my own. But I went with the safe choice. "I want to travel. I wish I could go to Alaska."

He raised a brow. "Alaska?

Tipping my head up, I laughed. "Yes." I met his waiting gaze again. "I've always wanted to go there."

"Hm. Gotcha. I'm just surprised you didn't say some place like Greece or Costa Rica. Some place with a beach and warm weather. I mean, if you want snow, we do live in Michigan."

I shoved him playfully. "Stop making fun of me. I do want to visit those places. Definitely. But I'd like to go to Anchorage."

"Why?"

Shrugging, I said, "I don't know. I just do. I'd also like to see the Northern Lights. Oh, and I want to visit some of the cultural attractions, ski, take a cruise on the Pacific. It sounds fun to me. Romantic."

"If you say so." He held up his glass. "Well, let's toast and agree. To cold ass Alaska."

Grinning, I touched my glass to his. "To Alaska."

I tasted the cider and moaned. "This is so good. You have a gift."

"It's my granny's recipe, with a few little tweaks."

I finished my drink and set the empty cup down on the table. "Yum. I'll have to take some home with me. I love it!"

"I'll make you some. For your birthday."

"It's almost over. Anyway, what about you? What would you wish for?"

"It's not my birthday," he teased. "This is all about you, remember?"

I pointed at him. "But you said I could ask you a question."

"Okay," he conceded. "If I could have one wish..." His gaze fell to my mouth. Inching closer until his knee bumped mine, he murmured, "I'd want a do-over."

My eyes were laser focused on his lips. "A do-over?"

"Yeah. A do-over."

Then, he kissed me. And, *oh God*, it might have been worth the wait. Because… *Shit.* He was good at this.

A low groan pierced the air. It was me. I knew it because with every brush of his lips against mine, every stroke of his tongue against mine, I was coming undone. Almost like he was taking me apart inch by delicious inch.

With our lips fused together, he pulled me onto his lap. "Juke," I breathed.

This man was turning me inside out, flipping everything I thought I knew about kissing on its head. And I never wanted to stop. I wanted to drench myself in Juke, spend the rest of my life exploring him.

"Ronnie," he murmured as he kissed a tender path along my jaw to my ear. "I want you." He bit down on my ear lobe before sucking it into his mouth.

Damn. He's hot. Blazing hot. Literally. My temperature had skyrocketed in a matter of seconds. My lips were tingling, my heart was racing. My skin… My eyes popped open. Itching? *Oh no.* I bucked up and slid my ass right to the ground. Jumping up, I frantically, scratched my neck. Then, my arms. And my legs. Oh, and my stomach. I lifted up my shirt. *Hives.*

Juke stood, concern in his brown eyes. "Ronnie, are you okay?"

I blinked. *Oh shit.* Clapping a hand over my mouth. *Please no.* I prayed my lips wouldn't swell up because I was having an allergic reaction to something. Was it him? *Please don't let me be allergic to him! I need an orgasm. Stat.*

He stepped forward.

I held my hands out to stop him. "Don't move."

"Ronnie, what's wrong?"

Maybe I'm panicking for no reason. I took a few calming breaths. Nope, I'm still itchy and hot and... *Dammit.*

"I get it. It was too fast." He backed up—all the way to the other side of the couch. "You're not ready? I understand."

I shook my head rapidly. "It's not you." I refused to move my hand from my mouth. "But... What was in that drink?"

He frowned. "Apples, cinnamon, cloves... And strawberries."

My eyes widened. "Strawberries? Oh no. I'm allergic."

The first time I'd eaten a strawberry, I was three-years old. My mom told me she had to rush me to the hospital because my entire face swelled up. The second time, I was thirteen. I'd decided to test the waters again because I wanted to eat the chocolate-covered strawberries my friend's mother had sent to our class for her birthday. I found out the hard way that strawberries... *Are. Not. For. Me.* And I learned that lesson after my entire class made up a new nickname for me. *Mrs. Potato Head.*

After that day, I vowed to never eat anything strawberry again. I didn't even use strawberry flavored lip gloss or burn strawberry scented candles. Oh, and raspberries? Too much like those devil strawberries. And I'd been careful about putting new things in my mouth. Until now. Until Juke had slipped me some of his cider.

Despite that hot ass kiss, this birthday officially sucked. I had to get the hell out of there before he saw my version of Mrs. Potato Head live and in full color. "I have to go. Good kiss. Thank you."

Then, I raced out of the sunroom.

"Ronnie?"

Shit, he's following me.

"Let me help you. I'll get you some Benadryl."

"No!" I yelled, now moving at a fast clip down the long hallway toward the bathroom. "Send Brooklyn. Please."

He caught up to me quickly. "I'm sorry, Ronnie. I didn't know you were allergic."

"It's okay. I'm fine." *Don't look at him.* I kept my eyes straight ahead. "Brooklyn. Can you find her?"

Parker rounded the corner at that moment. He frowned, eyeing Juke suspiciously. "What's going on?"

"Nothing!" I assured him.

"She's allergic to strawberries," Juke said. "I use them in my cider."

My big brother rushed over to me. "Need anything?"

"Brook. Lynn." I grumbled. Once I reached the bathroom, I opened the door. "Now." Before they could say anything else, I slammed the door, effectively shutting them both out. *Oh, God, make it stop!*

Chapter Four

SUFFERING BASTARD

JUKE

*S*ometime around my sixteenth birthday, right around the time my granddad had a fatal heart attack, I'd nearly destroyed my life because I was so angry. Angry at him for dying on me, angry at my granny for wanting to die with him, and angry at myself for buckling under the pressure.

The entire year that followed, I'd made it my mission to find trouble. As a result, I'd been hauled down to the Wellspring Sheriff's Office a time or two. Strangely enough, though, Sheriff Walker never arrested me, probably because he felt sorry for me.

The few times I'd had to sit in the small interrogation room at the precinct, face-to-face with one of the deputies, I kind of felt like I did at this exact moment.

Three minutes. Two pairs of eyes. One skeptical. One amused.

Ronnie had slammed the door in my face. Literally. Since she'd barricaded herself in the bathroom, I'd been questioned by her brothers—my friends—like I'd committed a crime.

"Someone should probably go get Brooklyn," I suggested. "Your sister needs that medicine."

Parker looked at Bryson, then back at me. "Are you going to tell us what happened?"

"I already did." At least five times. "What the hell is this?"

Bryson smirked. "You trying to get with my sister?"

"So what if I am?"

That kiss earlier had been an appetizer, a prelude of sorts. And I couldn't wait to sample the main dish. Her. On my dick, in my bed, or anywhere else she wanted to go.

Bryson and I had been best friends since he'd moved to Wellspring years ago. I'd known him long enough to know that he wasn't really that bothered. But Parker... While I considered him a friend, he was a master at the poker face. Which was why he'd taken plenty of my money during our weekly card games.

"I distinctly remember a conversation we had twenty-something years ago about boundaries." Parker tilted his head, his eyes hard. "Sister off-limits. Right?"

I snorted. "Yeah, I remember. That was around the time Brooklyn started getting breasts."

Bryson snickered. "You noticed."

I shrugged. "I'm a man."

"Veronica is my sister, too," Parker said.

"And also a grown ass woman." I raised a challenging brow. "Correct?"

Parker pointed to the closed bathroom door. "She's important to us. We just want to make sure you under-stand... We're very protective."

I smiled. "Really? I didn't know that."

Bryson broke, barking out a laugh. He shoved Parker, who cracked up, too. "We're just playin' around."

"Maybe," Parker added.

"No sex in my house, though," Bryson warned. "Take that shit somewhere else."

Jordan stepped around the corner and leaned against the wall, sucking in a deep breath. "Why are y'all all the way back here?"

"I texted her to bring the medicine," Bryson announced.

"Damn, I'm outta breath," Jordan said. "I should've stopped eating when I was full instead of stuffing my face." She bent over at the waist. "Woo."

Bryson kissed his wife and took the Benadryl from her. "Thanks, bae." He glanced at me. "Do you want me to give it to Veronica?"

I snatched the medicine from him. "I'll handle it."

Jordan handed me the bottle of water she had in her other hand. "Take care of her, Juke. I have to get these kids in the bed so we can start game night." She waved and walked off.

I looked at Parker. "You got a problem with this?"

Parker raised his hands. "Nope." He clasped my shoulder. "You got it. Remember what I said, though."

I nodded. Once they left, I knocked on the bathroom door.

"Is Brooklyn out there?" Ronnie shouted.

"No."

"You can't come in," she said.

"Ronnie, come on. It can't be that bad."

The door flung open. Ronnie stood there, eyes wild, clothes disheveled, face... "Ooh."

Her eyes widened. "See!" She tried to slam the door

again, but I stopped it with my toe. "I look a hot mess, Juke." Closing her eyes, she sighed. "Not very sexy."

I pushed my way in and stood before her. Squeezing her shoulders, I told Ronnie, "You look beautiful."

She covered her mouth and averted her gaze. "Don't lie."

I cradled her face in my palms, forcing her to look at me. "Not lying. It's just a little swollen."

"A little? My lips look like punching bags."

Handing her the pills, I said, "It's nothing that a dose of Benadryl can't fix." I untwisted the cap off the bottle and gave it to her once she'd plopped the pills in her mouth.

"Thanks." She finished the water after a few minutes and sighed. "My night is officially done. I'll be sleep within an hour."

"I'll drive you home," I offered.

An hour later, after I basically snuck her out of the house, I pulled into her driveway. Turning to her, I smiled. She was asleep. I took a moment to catalog her face. Even with swollen lips and puffy cheeks, she was stunning. The more she let me into her world, the more I wanted to immerse myself into her. I hated to wake her, but I shook her gently. "Ronnie, wake up."

She jolted awake. "Huh?"

I squeezed her wrist. "We're here."

A wisp of a smile crossed her lips before she sagged back into the seat. "Okay." She closed her eyes.

Chuckling, I got out of my truck and jogged around to the passenger side. I opened the door and nudged her again. "Ronnie. Let's go."

Her eyes popped open and she grinned. "Are you real?"

"Very," I told her. "Come on."

It took several minutes for me to get her to the door because she kept stopping and patting her pockets for her keys—which I had because Brooklyn had given them to me before we left. After I ushered her inside, I unzipped her coat, took off her hat, and led her to the couch.

Ronnie grimaced as she scratched her legs. Mumbling something about itching and no clothes, she unbuttoned her jeans and pushed them off. *Damn.* Next, she took off her socks and threw them behind my head. She muttered something else, but I couldn't concentrate on her words when her painted toes, her bare legs and those white cotton panties had all of my attention. *Does she have on a matching bra?*

Before she could pull her shirt off, I stopped her. "Ronnie, you have company."

She glanced around. "Who is it?"

"Me?"

Waving a dismissive hand my way, she said, "You're not company. You've been here before."

True. I'd come to many group dinners and fight parties. I'd even helped her with her Christmas lights a few weeks ago. She'd always been fully dressed, though. And definitely not doped up on Benadryl.

She fell back on the cushions and curled up. I grabbed the blanket off of her recliner and spread it over her. Running a finger over her forehead, I asked, "Do you need anything?"

"Yes." She hugged a throw pillow. "A nap. And water."

Exhaling slowly, I made my way to the kitchen. I found her stash of Benadryl and took two bottles of water from the fridge. When I came back into the living room, she was snoring lightly.

I set the stuff down on the table next to the sofa. She opened her eyes and smiled. "You're good at this."

Frowning, I asked, "What?"

"Taking care of me. I think I'll keep you." Her eyes fluttered closed. "You should stay."

I dropped to my knees in front of her. "Do you need me to?"

"Huh?"

"Stay. Do you want me to stay?

Her eyes locked on mine. She reached out and brushed her thumb over my bottom lip. "If you want to."

"I'll stay for a little while."

She sighed contently. "Thanks." Frowning, she asked, "Are my lips still swollen?"

The Benadryl had done its work. Her mouth was only slightly swollen now. I suspected the itching would be a distant memory soon. "Not really."

"So I don't look like Mrs. Potato Head?"

I laughed. "Not even a little bit. Who told you that?"

"Long story," she grumbled. "I appreciate you for being here."

I stared at her, reveling in being near her. Tonight, we'd turned a corner and I wanted to stay on course. "I appreciate you, too. Now, get some sleep."

"Okay. Juke?"

"Yes, Ronnie."

Gripping my collar, she pulled me closer. "If you kiss me on my forehead again, I'll kick your ass."

I laughed softly. "I won't." Cupping her chin in my palm, I kissed her softly.

She moaned. "That's good. More of that, please."

Brushing my lips over hers again, I murmured. "Soon."

A few minutes later, she was sleep.

Chapter Five

GRANNY'S OLD FASHIONED

VERONICA

*M*ornings were my favorite part of the day. Usually, I started with a workout and a smoothie or yoga and a small breakfast. Today, though, I was late. I was supposed to have hit the road an hour ago, but I could barely get up. Must have been the antihistamine coupled with the embarrassment of yesterday.

I finally got my kiss, but there was no retiring to the bedroom for dirty sex. No breakfast in bed after sleepy sex. No shower sex before lunch. Just me, my swollen lips, and my Benadryl.

So, instead of starting the four-hour drive to Indianapolis, I ended up in front of Brook's Pub. Sighing, I hopped out of the car and walked to the door. The bar wasn't open this early, but I knew he'd be there. He was a morning person, too. And he was usually at work by eight.

I knocked on the door.

Seconds later, the door opened and Juke was standing there. He smiled. "Hey."

I'd gassed myself up the entire ride over, intent on apologizing for my dramatic overreaction in the sunroom. But now that he was in front of me, looking so fine in dark jeans and a long sleeved shirt rolled up at the sleeves, I couldn't seem to get my thoughts together.

He frowned. "Are you okay?"

I shook myself out of my thoughts. "I'm fine," I croaked finally. "Can I come in?"

Holding the door open, he gestured inside. "Come on."

"Thanks." I brushed past him and hurried toward the bar. Taking a seat on my favorite stool, I waited for him to join me.

He pulled out the chair next to mine and sat down. "How are you feeling?"

I shrugged my coat off and set it and my purse atop the bar. "Much better."

"Want something to eat? I just ordered breakfast from the Bees Knees." He glanced at his watch. "Should be here any minute."

"No, thanks. I have to leave soon. My mother is expecting me this afternoon."

"Oh, right. You're going to Indiana."

I sighed. "I wanted to stop by before I left. To thank you again for everything." I swallowed hard. "And to apologize."

With narrowed eyes, he asked, "Why would you apologize?"

"For acting deranged."

He chuckled, low and sexy-as-hell. The sound went straight to my pussy, like he was stroking my clit with his fingers or his tongue. Squeezing my legs together, I flattened a hand over my chest as a delicious shiver worked its way through my body.

"Ronnie?"

"Yes," I whispered.

"No need to apologize." He pulled my stool closer to him, so close our knees were touching. "But I'm glad you stopped by. I wanted to talk to you, too. About what happened."

"Before the swollen face or after?"

He searched my eyes. "Both."

Nodding, I told him, "Yesterday was the longest day ever. It felt like a whole week."

"Tell me about it," he agreed. "I wanted to explain myself, though."

Intrigued, I leaned forward. "Okay."

"I need to apologize to you, for leaving you hanging after the countdown. I never intended to give you that forehead kiss."

"Why did you?"

His shoulders fell. "Laura and I have... a weird and complicated history. And I knew that I had to put a period at the end of that long relationship before I kissed you, before I did anything with you. Because I don't want anything to come between us and what I see happening with us."

Slowly, I let out a breath I hadn't realized I was holding. "What do *you* see happening with us?"

"More than a New Year's kiss."

I smiled. "Do tell."

"I can talk to you about anything, but I can also be quiet with you."

I felt the same way about Juke. There was a comfort level between us that made being with him easy. Somehow, we usually gravitated toward each other at events. More often than not, we'd ended up partners during game nights. On bowling league nights, he always bought my French fries. Sitting in silence with him, laughing at everything or nothing, or even playing darts on a busy night at the bar felt normal. It felt right.

"Even though I value our friendship," he continued, "I think it's pretty clear that I don't have *just friends* feelings for you."

"I think we're on the same page."

"Alright. You go."

I lifted one shoulder. "Since we're being honest, I'll just say that I've never had a great relationship. There was always something holding me back. I realize now, it was me. I just let things happen, even if I didn't like it."

I worked through my senior prom because my boyfriend thought he could do better and asked my nemesis instead. My college boyfriend revealed he was gay after we'd dated for two years. I smiled through that heartbreak and had even hooked him up with his current husband. My first orgasm came courtesy of a sex toy—at age twenty-two. Never mind I'd been having sex for years with my small-dicked fiancé who'd slut-shamed me for wanting to try a position other than missionary.

"I don't want to live that way anymore," I continued. "At all. When I met you, I immediately felt a connection. I want to explore that."

"I like that. Now..." My gaze dropped to his hands, which were slowly inching up my legs. When he reached my thighs, he tugged me even closer, until I was nestled between *his* legs. His tongue darted out to moisten his lips. I was transfixed on the motion. "Allergic reaction aside, I'm thinking it might have been a good thing that we didn't take things too far."

"A good thing?" I asked, my eyes still glued to his

mouth.

"Admittedly, I'm a little old-fashioned in some ways."

I forced my gaze away from his mouth to his eyes. "So, what does that mean exactly?"

"It means…" He traced my bottom lip with his tongue. "I don't know if I could have stopped myself from stripping you naked and letting you throw yourself on my dick. Since you meant that shit," he added. "And I always want to give you what you want."

Oh shit. I dug my nails into his arms. A nervous giggle burst from my mouth. "I was definitely irritated when I said that."

"But I would like to take you out on a proper date before I…"

"Make me come?" I giggled when his eyes widened. "I'm kidding." I wasn't.

"Right." He arched a brow, like he didn't believe me. "So when you get back from visiting your mother, I'm taking you out. Just me and you. Dinner. Dessert."

"After dessert?" I whispered.

"Breakfast, too." Juke nipped my chin, before pulling me onto his lap for a kiss.

My heart pounded in my ears as he worked his magic with his talented lips, winding me up until I couldn't feel anything but him. He brushed his lips across my collarbone up to my ear.

"We need to stop," he murmured.

I leaned back. "Are you sure?"

He smirked. "Not really."

Groaning, I slid off of his lap and took a few deep breaths. The braids in my hair prevented me from pulling it out, but I mimicked the action anyway. "You're killing me."

He stood, grabbing the hem of my shirt and tugging

me back to him. "Believe me, I want this. Not in the middle of the bar, though."

"Fine." I pouted. "By the way, I'm not sex-crazed or anything. You're just hot."

Juke barked out a laugh. "You're funny."

I rolled my eyes. "I guess." Stepping on the tips of my toes, I kissed him. "I better go."

He picked up my coat. "Okay." Stepping behind me, he held it open until I slid my arms in the sleeves. When I turned around to face him, he zipped my coat up and put my hat on my head.

"Thanks." I grinned up at him. "You're such a gentleman."

He scratched his ear. "Sometimes." He winked.

I slipped a hand in his and he walked me to my car. Outside, he opened my door for me, waiting until I climbed in before closing it. Once I turned on the ignition, I rolled the window down. "I'll text you when I get there."

Leaning in, he placed a slow, lingering kiss to my lips. "Call me."

I gripped his collar, holding him in place. "You know the town will talk. I'm sure someone just saw you kiss me."

"Tomorrow, everyone will think we eloped because you were pregnant with my baby."

I giggled. "Or Laura hit you in the head with her shoe because she found out we were having an illicit affair behind her back."

He cracked up. "Right." He kissed me again. "I don't care, though." Stepping away from the car, he waved. "Drive safe."

As I drove away, I thought about last night, about the wish I'd made out loud and the silent ones I'd been too scared to voice. For the first time, I thought all of them might be within reach. And I couldn't be happier.

Chapter Six

SNOW IN THE CRACK

JUKE

"A gentleman would at least take a woman to dinner before he fucks her."

Growing up with a granny that had no filter had prepared me to handle anything. That particular piece of advice hadn't been asked for or received well. What fifteen-year-old kid wanted his grandmother to talk about fucking or anything related to his dick? But that didn't stop Julianne Lee Bush from saying anything she wanted to say —at any moment.

The lesson stuck with me, though. Which was why I didn't take anyone to bed lightly. Sure, I'd had my fair share of pussy, but for the most part, I didn't enjoy sleeping around. The older I got, the more I realized I wanted what Bryson had with Jordan, what Parker had with Kennedi, what Brooklyn had with Carter. I wanted to come home to

ELLE WRIGHT

someone at the end of the night. I looked forward to foot massages, middle-of-the-night sex... babies.

Is Ronnie that person for me? Sometimes I wondered if she was too good to be true, if she would morph into someone I couldn't stand—like Laura had. But the part of me that had fallen hard for Ronnie knew she was everything I thought she was.

In fact, the only doubt I had now was... *Italian or Steak-house?* It had been a week since I'd asked her out on a date. Officially. While she was in Indianapolis, we'd talked often. We'd even eaten dinner together on a Zoom chat.

One night, she'd called me in tears because of some family thing. I spent hours trying to make her laugh. Eventually, we watched a movie together on Netflix. She'd fallen asleep, though. And I'd listened to her soft snores until I did, too.

Early this morning, she'd texted me to let me know she was on her way home. I'd responded with an invitation to dinner. Whether we ended up in her bed tonight or mine remained to be seen, but I would be lyin' if I said I didn't want to be with her. My hands itched to explore her body in ways that I'd dreamed about. But I'd let her set the pace. I was down for whatever *she* wanted. Because my granny had taught me gentlemanly manners.

If only the weather would hold up.

The bell above the door rang, and I looked up to see Mr. Mays had shuffled in, covered in snow. "Hey, Old Man," I called.

"Juke! How the hell are ya?" he asked, shaking his hat off. "It's cold out there."

Carl Mays had owned CM Market for years, until the local Walmart put him out of business. His wife, Mildred, and my granny were best friends. And they'd died within months of each other. We'd supported each other through that time, and I continued to be there for him whenever he needed me.

I poured him his usual. Grapefruit juice on ice. No gin. "What are you doing out today?"

At eighty-years-old, Mr. Mays was still on the go, driving his pick-up truck through town, walking his dog in the park every single day. "Looks like we're going to get a snow storm," he mused, taking a sip of his drink. "Six to eight inches. I came down here to get a few things, in case I'm snowed in for a few days."

Frowning, I picked up my phone and checked the forecast. Sure enough, what had started out as scattered flurries had now been upgraded to a damn-near blizzard. *Shit*.

I leaned my elbows against the bar. "Hopefully, it passes by."

"You know how it is, son. We live in Michigan."

Chuckling, I nodded at a couple as they walked out of the bar. "Have a good evening," I told them. My waitress was on lunch, so I hurried to their table to clean it off.

I set the couple's used dishes in a bin and wiped the table off. On my way back to the bar, I asked Mr. Mays, "Need me to help you with anything? You still have Sheriff Walker's grandson taking care of your home maintenance?"

"I'm fine," he grumbled. "You need to worry about yourself."

I blinked. "Huh? Something I should know?"

Mr. Mays eyed me curiously. "You heard me."

I lifted my shoulders. "I have no idea what you're talking about, Old Man."

"You know people talk. I just heard something, that's all."

I sighed. Since New Year's, I'd been hearing all kinds

of rumors about me, about me and Laura, about me and Ronnie, about Ronnie and Laura. "What did you hear?"

He shrugged. "That you got the Wells girl pregnant. Laura found out and stole all your shit before she left town."

Of course, that was what he'd heard. I laughed. "Yeah, no. That's not what happened."

"You and the Wells gal… is that true?"

"Maybe," I admitted.

Mr. Mays grinned. "Boy, I might be old but I can still whoop your ass."

Laughing, I said, "I like her. We're seeing what happens."

"Well, I'll be damned. You finally got your head out of your ass and asked her out, huh? I knew you were sweet on her."

Curious, I asked, "How did you know?"

"Because I see the way you look at her. Like I looked at Mil. Take it from me, if you find someone that will hold all of your attention, don't let go."

Nothing he'd said was untrue. It only served as a confirmation for me. "Thanks for the advice."

"Anytime, son." Mr. Mays stood. "Let me get out of here."

I walked him to the door. "Be careful out there. Text me when you get home."

"Will do. Aren't you proud of me? I'm getting good at this technology thing."

I smiled, remembering the day I'd tried to teach him about texting. That hours-long lesson was frustrating as hell. But it was worth it, just to get that quality time.

"That's good," I told him. "Maybe next time I could teach you how to order your groceries and have them delivered."

He waved me off. "I'm not doing that shit. I need to get out of the house every now and then. Going grocery shopping counts as exercise according to my grand-daughter."

"True."

"See you soon." He stepped down onto the sidewalk. "Bye, now."

I watched him walk to his car and waited until he drove off before I closed the door. I peered up at the sky. One thing was sure… I needed a contingency plan for dinner. I placed a few calls and made a quick run to the store.

I'd just made it back to the bar when my phone buzzed.

Ronnie: *I need help.*

I paused, wondering if she'd made it back home. The roads were probably slick heading into town. I replied: *Are you okay?*

A few minutes later, another text came through: *I'm stuck. Can you come?*

I texted that I was on my way and asked her to send me her location. Once I let my staff know that I was out for the rest of the day, I left.

Several minutes later, I pulled next to Ronnie's car. It had taken twice as long to get to her, due to the icy driving conditions. But I spotted her right away. She was about a mile away from her neighborhood. Judging by the angle of her car, she'd slid off the road, most likely due to the sheet of ice under the falling snow.

I veered off the road and parked in front of her. More than likely, I'd have to pull her car out of the little ditch she was in.

She jumped out of the car. "You're here! Thank God."

It took half an hour for me to get her car out of the ditch. Then, I followed her home. I helped her pull her luggage out of the car. The snow was coming down fast. Big, fat flakes covered the ground, ensuring any plans I had this evening would be canceled.

One thing about living in Wellspring? The people here didn't play about the snow. Downtown restaurants closed, schools dismissed early, and residents were content to stay indoors.

My phone buzzed. I read the new text message and was relieved to see that Mr. Mays had made it home. Dropping it back in my coat pocket, I grinned at Ronnie who was slowly inching her way toward me.

"You wore the wrong shoes," I told her, looking down at her boots. They were for fashion, not for ice.

Ronnie rubbed her gloved hands together. "Looks like it's going to get worse."

"Yeah," I grumbled, unable to keep the irritation out of my voice.

"No dinner, huh?"

I shook my head. "Looks that way." I took off my glove and brushed a snowflake from her cheek.

"Thanks for coming to get me." She smirked. "I thought I was doing something taking the side roads. I thought it would be quicker, less traffic. I can drive in snow, but damn... this shit is not for me."

"Do me a favor." I picked up the suitcases. "Next time you get the urge to take a shortcut in a blizzard, don't." I stalked off to the door. I was right in front of the stairs when I felt a blast of wet, icy, snow against my neck. Dropping the suitcases, I whirled around.

With narrowed eyes on me and another snowball in hand, Ronnie said, "How about this? Next time you try to tell me what to do, remember this moment, and don't."

I ducked right before a ball of snow whizzed passed by my head and splattered on the side of the house. But I wasn't quick enough for the second one, which hit me right on my forehead.

"Oh, you're going to get it now." I picked up a mound of snow, forming a snowball quickly.

She flung another one at me, barely missing me. "I'm not scared." Then, she took off, running around the house into the backyard."

I raced to catch up with her, throwing snow as I ran and dodging flying snow from her. Finally, I reached her, wrapping my arms around her waist and picking her up. She laughed, her head falling back as I twirled her around. But I'd forgotten one thing... wet snow was slippery. And before I could correct myself, I tumbled over, falling straight on my back.

Ouch. I winced as pain shot through my lower back. But she was still laughing, probably because she'd landed on me and not on the cold ground.

She looked at me, her eyes dancing with amusement. "Are you okay?"

"I'm...good."

Ronnie rolled off of me onto her back. We stayed like that for a little while, just watching the snow fall on us.

"I love the snow," she confessed. "Especially fresh snow." I heard her shift and turned to find her staring at me. "When I was a kid, I made a snowman every year. And I loved making snow angels." Smiling, she opened her mouth. "And it tastes so good." She inhaled. "It smells good, too."

Frowning, I said, "Does snow have a smell?"

"Of course, it does. If you really pay attention."

I took a deep breath. It was subtle, but it did have a soft scent to it. *Or maybe it's her.*

"My granny loved the snow, too."

A familiar pang of sadness squeezed my heart. There

wasn't a day that passed that I didn't think of her. The strongest woman I'd ever known. I don't think I'd ever seen her shed a tear, not even when my mother—her only child —died of cancer before the age of thirty. Granny had simply planned the funeral, filed for legal guardianship, and went to work the next day.

Years later, I realized she'd drowned all of her sorrows in alcohol. A gin and tonic here, a martini there, a glass of wine with dinner. The first drink I'd ever made was a Tom Collins—Seagrams Gin, maple syrup, lemon juice, and soda water. It was her favorite and I was happy to oblige her because I didn't know any better.

In my early twenties, I'd come home from college with a busted knee and a desire to open my own bar. The journey hadn't been easy, but she'd cheered me on and made me promise never to give up. I made her promise to stop drinking if I ever made my dream a reality.

The day Brook's Pub opened, we celebrated. The next morning, she went to her first AA meeting and eventually became one of Wellspring's top AA sponsors. For the rest of her life, she'd spent her time helping others put the liquor down. Kind of ironic I'd built a career serving drinks to paying customers. But she'd always told me that not everyone carried the liquor cross, and it was important to let people make their own choices. She was the reason I stayed away from the hard stuff and never let my customers drink themselves into a stupor. I considered it my personal mission. For her.

"I wish I could have met her," she said softly. "From what you've told me, she was a phenomenal woman."

"She was."

"She raised you. And you're a good guy."

"She pushed me. So hard. I wouldn't be where I am without her."

Too bad Granny wasn't here to bask in my success with me. Before she died, though, she'd begged me to open my heart to someone special, someone who wouldn't use me for what I could give them, someone who'd love me unconditionally. As I stared into Ronnie's eyes, feelings I'd never felt before took over and I knew that person was her.

"She would've liked you," I continued. *I like you.* I more than liked her.

Ronnie squeezed my hand. A few minutes later, she asked, "Cold yet?"

"Been cold." Moving closer, I nuzzled my nose against her neck. "But you're right. I like the smell of snow...on you."

She giggled, wrapping her arms around my shoulders. "I think I missed you."

I squeezed her waist until she dissolved into laughter again. "You think?" Meeting her gaze, I whispered, "I know I missed you."

Brushing my cheeks with her thumbs, she kissed me. It was cold as hell, wet, and dark, but I'd never felt so warm, so alive. So open to any and everything with her.

Chapter Seven

HOP, SKIP, AND GO NAKED

VERONICA

*P*laying in the snow with Juke was my favorite part of the week. After my trip to Indianapolis, I'd needed the reprieve. And standing there, wrapped in the warm cocoon of his embrace, rocking back and forth to the music in our hearts, I felt safe.

I peered up at him. "Thanks for this."

He rubbed my shoulders. "I think I should be the one thanking you," he said, his voice almost a whisper.

Tonight, he'd shared more of his granny with me, which made me happy. I loved learning about his struggles and his triumphs. Because they'd made him who he was. A strong, capable, dependable, loyal, sexy man. *My man.*

It had taken forever for us to get out of the snow and make our way into the house. But he'd immediately turned on my fireplace, pulled my trusty blanket off of my chair and wrapped it around me, to warm me up. But the heat of the fireplace, the warmth of the blanket had nothing on him. His ability to calm me and arouse me started a flame in my gut that spread out to every part of me.

He searched my eyes and ran a finger down the side of my face. "How are you?"

"Better now."

"Did you get to talk to your mother?"

I sighed. "Not really. I kind of just left it alone, ya know?"

My nightmare trip was one for the record books. Between question after question about husband prospects, my spiritual walk, and my teaching career, I couldn't catch a break. The straw that had broken the camel's back was the massive argument I had with my mother and her husband. Over my ex-fiancé of all people. Apparently, his marriage was over and he'd been inquiring about me. My mother thought I was being absolutely unreasonable for not taking his calls.

Hell no was my answer when she'd approached me with an invitation to dinner—for a double date. I'd never cussed at my mother, not even in her presence. The words had slipped out as if I had no control over my tongue. Needless to say, that had opened an entire floodgate of accusatory statements, tears, and threats of leaving and never coming back. All of those things coming from me.

"I wanted to fix it," I explained. "I just couldn't get over how she'd let her husband treat me."

The night of the big blow-out, my mother's husband —*a man who was not my father*—berated me for the better part of an hour because I dared to push back against their expectations of me and my behavior while in *their* house. That was rich, considering my mother had purchased that same house with money *Senior* had given her. Because she'd agreed to never tell his wife—or anyone else—about me.

I plopped down on the couch, tucking my legs underneath my bottom. "The crazy part? While he was yelling at me, I stood there and let him because I was waiting for her to defend me."

My mother... She hadn't said a word. Not a *single* word. Which led to other choice words from me to both of them right before I'd stormed out. That night, I'd stayed in a hotel room and Juke had calmed my nerves. He always helped me find my way through the clutter. Whether I was sitting at the bar telling him about a decision I made or I was telling him a deep, dark secret.

He sat next to me. "Did she apologize to you when you went back?"

I nodded. "She did. And she told me she loved me." By then, it was too late. The damage had already been done. "But I don't think I'll go back there anytime soon."

Pulling me into his embrace, he pressed his lips to my temple. "I'm sorry."

I snuggled into him, loving the way we were with each other. "It is what it is. I told her I loved her, and that I'd always be there if she needed me. Then, I left."

We sat quietly for a few minutes. Until my stomach growled.

Sitting up straight, I patted my stomach and laughed. "I'm hungry. And I have *no* food."

He winked. "Luckily, I thought of everything." Without another word, he ran outside to his truck. Moments later, he came back with a bunch of bags in his hands. "Dinner."

A couple hours later, we were seated on the floor in front of the fireplace. I'd laid my blanket down and poured us some red wine. Juke hadn't lied when he'd told me he came prepared. He'd brought reinforcements, groceries for the week. We'd prepared a quick dinner together— spaghetti and meatballs, garlic bread and a tossed salad.

"Dinner was delicious." I took a sip of wine. "You really did think of everything."

He grinned. "I had a feeling the weather wouldn't cooperate with my plans."

"What exactly did you have planned?"

He studied me over the rim of his glass. His heated gaze flickered down to my lips before slowly traveling lower. And lower. When his eyes locked on mine again, he said, "I'll save it for another time."

I let out a shaky breath. "Question."

"What is it?"

"So… In your plans, did you envision spending the night?"

The half-smile, half-smirk he blessed me with made my heart race. "Ronnie." He gripped my thighs and pulled me to him. Leaning down, he brushed his lips over mine. "Do you want me to stay?"

Oh my. I nodded. "But I thought you were old-fashioned," I blurted out.

He laughed. "I am. I wanted to take you out, wine and dine you. Spoil you."

"You already do," I said. "I've never had anyone take care of me the way you do."

"You make me want to take care of you." He brushed my stomach with his thumb. "Ronnie, if I stay, things won't be the same tomorrow. I'm not the guy who fucks and flees."

"Good."

"This means something to me," he admitted. "*You* mean something to me."

"I feel the same way." I smirked. "Juke, today was perfect. Starting with you riding to my rescue, all the way up to this moment. And, hopefully, beyond." Juke kissed me then. Devoured me really—with his mouth, with his tongue. When he eased back, I pulled him forward and into another kiss. "Thanks for being such a gentleman. But just in case you need to hear this, I'm completely okay with skipping the fancy dinner on the town and getting to the hot sex part."

"You're so beautiful." Juke nuzzled my cheek. "I can't believe how lucky I am."

"Oh my God, you're killing me!" I grumbled, slipping my hand under his shirt. I scraped my fingers over his stomach, enjoying the way his muscles flexed under my touch. "You keep saying things that make me want you more."

He tugged at the hem of my shirt. "Take this off," he commanded softly.

Ah, shit. I cheered in my head as I lifted my shirt up and off, tossing it behind me somewhere.

His warm lips traveled over the bridge of my nose, down to my chin, then, my neck. He traced the fabric of my bra with his tongue, pulled it down and scraped one of my nipples with his teeth before sucking it into his mouth. Oh, but he didn't stop there. He brushed his mouth over my stomach, dipping his tongue in my belly button. I heard the sound of my zipper, but it didn't register that he was sliding my pants off until I felt his breath on my legs.

His hands were everywhere, but his tongue… *Oh God.* Masterful. I was helpless to formulate a coherent thought that didn't involve him. My body was a livewire, ready to blow at any moment.

Juke kissed his way back up my body to my lips. He settled between my thighs and deepened the kiss. I moaned when he brushed his hand over my core. I purred when he slipped one finger—then another—inside my pussy. I trembled when he pressed his thumb to my clit. And I screamed when a delicious orgasm rolled through me.

When I could finally breathe normally again, I opened my eyes. He stared at me, an amused smile on his perfect lips. I tugged at his shirt. "Take this off," I ordered saucily, tossing his earlier command back at him.

He chuckled, shaking his head. "I think I want you to do it." He rolled off of me, pulling me on top of him.

Straddling his lap, I unbuttoned his shirt slowly, kissing the expanse of his chest as I did. I winked at him, before I took his pants and boxer briefs off, intent on tasting him. But he pulled on my braids lightly, halting my movement. My gaze locked on his.

"I want you on my dick," he whispered. "Now."

Grinning, I climbed on top of him, rubbing against his erection until he groaned.

"Condom. Wallet. In. My. Pocket," he said, though clenched teeth.

I scrambled to pick up his jeans, my nerves raw and the anticipation killing me. He helped me, taking the pants from me, grabbing his wallet, and pulling the condom wrapper out. I snatched the condom from him and sheathed him, then lowered myself onto him. Slowly.

"Damn," we both said at the same time.

He sat up, unhooking my bra. Now we were skin-to-skin, connected in every way possible.

"Shit," he groaned pushing into me. Harder. Deeper. "You feel so good."

My mouth fell open on a wordless sigh. *Finally*. Feeling him against me, pulsing inside me, was enough to send me over the edge right then and there. But I wanted this to last. We stayed like that for a moment, giving me time to adjust to his size.

Soon, I rocked into him signaling I was ready. We started slow, lips fused together, arms wrapped around each other, moving to a rhythm that seemed innate. Like we were meant to be like this with each other. With each thrust, I surrendered all the tiny, broken pieces of myself to him. With each thrust, he slowly put them back together again.

I didn't want it to end, but I was teetering on the edge, unraveling. The pace quickened. He pushed, I pulled. He gave, I took. And when I came, I came long and hard. So hard, tears spilled from my eyes. He followed soon after, groaning my name over and over again.

Collapsing against him, I giggled. "That was so much better than that damn forehead kiss."

He fell back against the blanket, laughing. "I can see I'll never live that down."

I lifted myself up, grinning at him. "Never," I teased.

Juke ran a finger over my bottom lip. "I can also see I'm going to have to spend a lot of time making it up to you."

I wiggled my ass, loving that he was getting hard for me again. "Yes, please."

"Careful now," he warned. "You might be starting something you're not ready to finish."

"I'm definitely ready. For everything."

He placed a gentle kiss on my lips. "In that case," he smacked my ass, "I want a do-over."

As we began the dance again, making love our way, I realized... *I never want him to stop.*

Chapter Eight

TIE ME TO THE BEDPOST... FOREVER

VERONICA

*S*ometime in March

I groaned. "Don't stop."

Juke pushed into me, taking me from behind, making love to me in a way only he could. "I'll never stop," he whispered against my ear. He brushed a finger over my clit.

Above our heads, the Northern Lights danced across the sky. It was perfect. Stargazing, the unique backdrop, and him.

"Come for me, Ronnie. I need you."

I. Need. You. The magic words. I cried out his name as my orgasm shook through me. Soon, he was right with me.

I turned around in his arms. Grinning, I whispered, "It's still dark."

"Not for long." He tipped my chin up with his finger and kissed me. "What do you want to do tomorrow?"

I shrugged, burrowing into his warm body. "You. And eat."

"I think that can be arranged."

It was our third night in Alaska. Juke had surprised me with first class tickets for a seven-day trip to *The Last Frontier* state. We'd spent the first night in Anchorage, then took a short flight to Fairbanks. He'd thought of everything. I didn't have to do anything but show up.

From our private fiberglass "igloo", we had an amazing view of the Aurora Borealis. Although there were plenty of activities to do, we'd mostly stayed in and enjoyed each other. Our igloo had everything we needed—a bed, a bath-room, and a few other amenities.

I traced his goatee. "This is amazing, baby."

I peered at the sky, through the curved windows. The lights moved quickly. Flashes of different colors—blue, green, pink, purple—stretched across the sky. It seemed endless.

Emotion clogged my throat. "Beautiful," I murmured, my eyes riveted to the scene above me.

Juke had given me a once-in-a-lifetime vacation. He was my own personal genie-in-a-bottle, granting my every wish. He rarely took time off. That he would take an entire week off for this meant the world to me.

I tore my gaze away from the lights. "I can't thank you enough for bringing me here."

His eyes softened. "You should know by now that I'd literally do anything for you."

I knew that. He'd proven it time and again, in ways that I'd never even imagined. For me, it was the little things. It was the way he made my coffee in the mornings or how he knew when I needed a foot rub or a listening ear.

Over the last few months, we'd created our own rules for our lives—together and apart. No expectations. We'd just lived in the moment and enjoyed our time together. But I felt like we were on the precipice of something else. I

64

couldn't put my finger on it, but I knew things were about to change soon. I wasn't scared, though. In fact, it was just the opposite. I was ready.

Last month, I decided to leave my job at Wellspring Water Corp., with Parker's blessing, to start my own business as an Educational Consultant. One of the reasons I went into teaching was to positively impact kids. I'd missed that part of my life.

"Ronnie?"

His voice brought me out of my reverie. I smiled. "Yes."

"What are you thinking about?"

"I'm so grateful for this moment, for this time with you. I've had so many firsts since I left Indiana. But this... This will go in the record books as one of my top experiences."

"You don't have to keep thanking me, Ronnie. I love seeing the world through your eyes. I love you."

I gasped. "What?"

"I've lost a lot in my life. My parents, my grandparents. I don't let people in easily. But, somehow, I knew it was safe to let *you* in, to open my heart to you, to trust you with it. I don't regret that decision at all. You make me laugh, sweetie. You let me cry. You listen to me, even when I'm not talking. I'm so in love with you." He cupped my cheek with his palm. "I love your wit. I love that you call me out on my shit. I love that you're comfortable with me. I love that I make you nervous sometimes. I love your laugh. I love that you're dramatic. I love that you care about my feelings. I love that you don't try to change me. I love that you apologize when you're wrong. I love that you accept apologies when you're right. I love that you love to play in the snow."

His words... My response lodged in my throat. Because

I knew that if I said anything right now, it would come out more like a sob than a sentence.

"On your birthday," he continued, "you told me that you'd never had anything *just* for you."

I giggled nervously, swallowing past the lump in my throat. "I did," I managed to get out. Because he'd just told me he loved me and my heart was beating out of control with that revelation.

He grabbed my hand and placed it against his heart. His heartbeat was strong, and in sync with mine. "Feel that? This is just for you. *I'm* just for you. Making sure your wishes come true is my pleasure—and my promise." A tear finally fell from my eyes and he wiped it away with the pad of his thumb. "You're my moon and my stars. You're my sun. *You* matter to me."

"Oh, God." I was ugly crying now. That conversation in the sunroom seemed like a lifetime ago, but he'd remembered everything I'd said. And while we'd only been together for a few short months, I knew I loved him with everything in me.

"Some might think we're moving too fast, but I only care about what *you* think."

I drew in a shaky breath. "Juke, I…" I swallowed. "You started out as my bartender, then you became my friend. Now, you're my everything. It's not too fast. I don't know how it happened, but I'm so glad it did. I love you, too. I'm for *you*."

He cradled my head in his hands and pulled me into a tender kiss. Resting his forehead against mine, he said, "Good. I'm glad we're on the same page."

"We totally are," I agreed. "And you know what else?"

"What is it?"

"I'm happy now."

One More Drink

BROOK'S PUB
BAR MENU
FAVORITES

SET THE NEW YEAR ON FIRE

LONG ISLAND NO TEA

JUKE'S WINTER CIDER

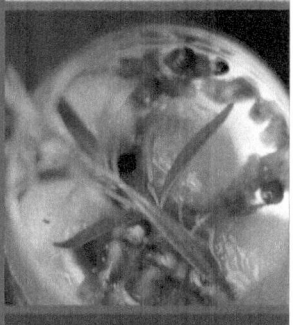

SUFFERING BASTARD

GRANNY'S OLD FASHIONED

SNOW IN THE CRACK

HOP, SKIP, AND GO NAKED

TIE ME TO THE BEDPOST

New Year Bae-Solutions

Eight Naughty Nights by Nicole Falls

Seven Month Drought by Sherelle Green

Six More Minutes by A.C. Arthur

Five Midnight Moments by Sheryl Lister

Four Page Letter by Angela Seals

Three Wrong Dates by Kelsey Green

Two Hot Kisses by Yahrah St. John

One More Drink by Elle Wright

Her Little Secret

Sex therapist, Paityn Young, couldn't get much sex in her city. So she developed her own line of naughty toys to get the job done. Now, she's bringing her talent to LA, hoping to launch her new company. Only her new business consultant has her thinking about more than just her product line.

As a favor to his boss, Bishop Lang agrees to help Paityn develop her new business. The only thing he knows about her is that she's off limits, but the moment he sees her, he realizes staying away might be harder than he thought. And his own personal journey may take a backseat to the blossoming relationship developing between them.

Excerpt: Her Little Secret

WOMEN OF PARK MANOR

*I*f Paityn could ban two words, *fuck* and *shit* would be it. One made her think of toilets. The other? Well, let's just say she didn't need to be reminded of something she hadn't been blessed to do in years. And for the last ten minutes, she'd listened to her sister string those same two words together in varying combinations.

"Girl! Enough!" Paityn shouted, cutting her sister off mid-curse. "Road rage is really a thing. Get help." Pulling two sets of new sheets out of the dryer, she walked into one of the spare bedrooms and dropped the bedding on the mattress.

"Shit, I need to vent," Blake yelled. "It's your fuckin' fault I'm in this predicament. Michigan traffic doesn't make me want to kill someone."

Unable to help herself, Paityn giggled at her younger sister's antics. "You're a mess."

"Hey, I can only be me," Blake said.

The loud blare of the car horn followed by another colorful curse had her shaking her head in amusement. Some things would never change. Trump was still an asshole, she still couldn't eat beans to save her life, and Blake Young still had a potty mouth.

"I'm hanging up," Paityn told her sister. "I have stuff to do before you get here."

When "the brats" told her they were coming for a visit during the Memorial Day holiday, Paityn was ecstatic. Since her cross-country move, she'd seen her sisters countless times thanks to technology. But air kisses and virtual hugs didn't replace real face-to-face contact.

"Paityn?" Bliss called through the phone. She noted the rasp in her baby sister's voice, as if she'd been sleeping. "Are you making something for dinner? I'm hungry."

"Yes, ma'am." She walked the other set of sheets to the third bedroom and dumped them on the bed. "I'm making reservations. At this new Cuban restaurant Rissa told me about."

"Damn," Bliss muttered. "Will you at least cook breakfast in the morning?"

"You're so greedy," Blake said. "You just ate a whole foot-long sub and half of mine."

"I can't help it," Bliss shouted.

"I'm starting to think you're only here because you want me to cook for you." Paityn hurried to the kitchen and opened the oven. The homemade peach cobbler she'd prepared was almost done, Blake's favorite.

"No, I'm here because I miss you," Bliss said, just as Blake shouted another obscenity at a driver.

"That's good to hear." She also checked the macaroni and cheese baking in the bottom oven. *My favorite*.

"I wish Dallas could have come," Bliss mused. "I tried to get her to cancel her plans."

Paityn lifted the top off the pot on the stovetop, stirring the mustard and turnip greens a bit before she turned down the heat. "I do, too. But I'm not mad at her for taking a vacation out of the country. It's about time." She glanced at the Instant Pot on the countertop, noting the remaining time on the pulled pork, Bliss' favorite.

The truth? She did have reservations for dinner and dancing. Tomorrow. But, tonight, she also wanted to spoil her sisters a little. And it had been a while since she'd cooked anything of substance.

Growing up the second oldest child of a world-renowned couple, known for mending relationships and teaching others to parent, had a unique set of challenges. Partly because it was hard to live in her parents' shadows, but mostly because there were eight of them. Yes, Stewart and Victoria Young had eight damn children—willingly and happily. Paityn was the responsible sister, the oldest daughter, always offering a plate of food, a hand to hold, and a shoulder to cry on.

"Duke is pissed you didn't invite him," Bliss said.

Paityn laughed, thinking of the phone call she'd received from her brother earlier that morning. "I didn't invite y'all."

"But you're glad we're here," Blake added.

"I am, but I'm hanging up. I gave the concierge your names, so you should be able to come up without any problems. Don't kill anybody, Blake. See you soon."

Paityn ended the call after her sisters screamed good-bye. Shaking her head, she turned the dishwasher on and poured a glass of wine. When the oven timer went off, she pulled the dessert out and set it atop the island. The smell of peaches and cinnamon wafted to her nose and she resisted the urge to taste the cobbler.

She scanned the notes she'd jotted down earlier that day. The clitoral cream she'd hoped to perfect had been harder than she originally thought. Between her work as a sex therapist and her science background, it should have been a no brainer. Yet, she'd failed to even achieve the big "O" for the first two batches she'd made. Biting her thumbnail, she pondered her choice of ingredients. Maybe she'd used too much sodium benzoate?

Paityn scribbled an idea on the notepad and eyed the prototype she'd created. It was the fifth dildo she'd created and, by far, the best. She couldn't wait to show Blake and Bliss, which was why it was out in the open and not in her makeshift office-slash-lab.

Once Paityn had decided every woman needed a big ass dick, the wheels started spinning and a business idea formed. Paityn knew there were other sex aids on the market, entire stores dedicated to the business of pleasure, but she'd jumped in anyway. Now she was preparing to pitch her brand of sexual enhancement products.

When her stomach growled, Paityn glanced over at the peach cobbler. *One spoonful won't hurt.* She grabbed a wooden spoon and scooped a heaping helping out of the pan. Before she knew it one bite turned into two. Then, three. *Oh my God.* Four.

Fortunately, the knock on the door interrupted her greedy moment. She licked the spoon as she headed toward the door. She'd figured it would be at least thirty minutes before her sisters arrived. The airport was less than fifteen miles away, but it almost always took more than thirty minutes to get there in the infuriating 405 traffic.

She wiped a hand against her black leggings and opened the door. "You're her—"

Only it wasn't Blake or Bliss at the door. It wasn't even Rissa. No, the very *male* visitor standing there, his fist poised to knock again, was someone she didn't know. But damn, he was someone she probably *should* get to know.

Swallowing, she plastered a grin on her face and hoped

she looked presentable. "Hi." When he didn't answer immediately, she swallowed. *Maybe the hottie is a creeper?* But it wasn't like she was in some random apartment building. The concierge didn't just let anyone come up to the top floor.

The stranger's eyes dropped to her mouth and she absently wiped it with her sleeve, hoping she didn't have peach cobbler crust on her face.

"Can I help you?" she asked.

He blinked and then blessed her with the sexiest smile she'd ever seen up close. Pretty white teeth, adorably deep dimples, and beautiful creases framing full lips.

"I'm sorry. My name is Bishop." He held out a hand, presumably for her to shake it.

Her gaze dropped to it, noted his long fingers and clean fingernails, but she made no move to touch him. *Not yet.*

"I work at Pure Talent," he continued. "Jax Starks told me about you."

Paityn's eyes widened. "Oh, yeah. Bishop Lang."

Why is my voice so high? Probably because when her godfather told her he wanted her to meet one of the best legal minds on his team, she'd assumed it was an old, graying grandfather. A man that golfed on his off days and spent weekends at some highbrow country club drinking Burnt Martinis or scotch on the rocks. Not this fine ass man with smooth dark skin and a body that made her want to sing, "Do me, Baby". Because she was sure he'd be able to handle the job in a way no one ever had before. *Focus, Paityn.*

"Yes, that's me." His tongue darted out to wet his lips. "I live in the building and figured I'd come up and intro-duce myself."

Unable to turn away, she nodded. "Right. I think Uncle Jax did tell me that."

Briefly, she wondered if this was even a good idea, considering she couldn't stop staring at him. How would she be able to concentrate on business? But she trusted her godfather's judgment because he had never failed her and always had her best interests at heart.

From an early age, Paityn learned that blood didn't make family. And it was because of relationships like the one her father and Jax Starks had. The two men had grown up near each other in Detroit, Michigan and had even pledged the same fraternity. They were brothers in every sense of the word, even though they were born to different parents. Jax was her godfather, but he was also her "uncle".

She finally stepped aside. "Come in."

He followed her toward the kitchen. "Peach cobbler." The low groan that followed hit her right in the gut—or lower. "Smells good."

She gulped down the rest of her wine and dropped the wooden spoon into the sink. "I'm making dinner for my sisters." She turned the greens off and tried to recall everything her godfather had told her about Bishop. Clearly, she'd missed some things that he'd said. "I thought you were going to be out of town until next week?"

"I got back a little early."

Paityn leaned against the counter, meeting his intense gaze once again. "Cobbler?" she asked.

He looked down at the dessert and swallowed visibly. Nodding slowly, he said, "No."

Paityn frowned, surprised at his answer. Normally, a nod meant yes. "You sure? Because you look like you want some."

"I'm sure." He glanced at the pan again, before he looked up at her.

Tilting her head, she studied him. Something was preventing him from eating her cobbler. Did she want to know what? *Or who?* The need to know more welled up inside her. *It's the nature of my job to ask questions.* It wasn't his arms. Or the muscles stretching against the t-shirt he wore. The fact that he may be eating someone else's pie didn't bother her either. Well, not really.

Instead of probing further, she decided a change of subject was best. "Uncle Jax tells me you work in the business development department," she said. "But what else should I know?" Okay, so her attempt to sound professional came out more sultry than businesslike.

"What do mean?" he asked.

Clearing her throat, she added, "Because if we're going to work together, I'd like to learn a little more about your ass." Her eyes widened. "I mean, your experience?"

He chuckled. "I can give you the long version, or the short version."

Hello, sexual innuendo. She really did need to get some. Everything about this man and this interaction made her mind sink to the gutter. Paityn scratched her neck. "How about we start with where you're from?"

"Long Beach."

She opened the refrigerator and pulled out two bottles of water and offered him one. "Law school?"

"Berkeley." He took the water and twisted off the cap. "I've worked for the agency for fifteen years, and I've been instrumental in negotiating several business deals for agency clients. Jax has also entrusted me with many of his personal business matters."

"Good. What has he told you about me?"

His mouth curved into a smile. "He mentioned you were important to him and that I should take care of you."

She bit down on her lip. "I mean, about my business idea."

"Only that you were a sex therapist looking to start a new venture."

Paityn grinned, pleased that he didn't seem uncomfortable with her occupation like some men. "That's true. Did he tell you anything else?"

Bishop raised a brow. "No. I assume you will tell me the details."

"Right. I'll send you the draft of my proposal." She slid her notebook over and jotted down a note to herself. "I probably should have done this as soon as he gave me your email address, but I didn't want to interrupt your vacation. I know we always say we won't check emails on vacation, but we always do."

Ha barked out a laugh. "I don't disagree with that."

"Let me know when you're free to meet." She closed the notebook. "I have appointments during the day, but I'm usually free in the evenings." Paityn conducted her sessions online, via video chat or text therapy, which she'd found to be a great alternative to in-office therapy. Most of her clients loved the convenience and it allowed her to work from the comfort of her home, wherever that was.

"I'll check my calendar and get back to you. I have your numbers."

"Great. You'll have an email tonight. Not that I don't think you wouldn't read my proposal before we meet, but you definitely should. And preferably not in the office. In front of people."

The last thing she wanted was for a picture of her prototype to flash across his screen while he had someone in his office. That would be embarrassing, for him and for her.

Bishop frowned. "Why do I feel like I should be scared?"

Paityn laughed. "Because you should." She waggled her eyebrows.

"Now, I'm curious. Maybe you should give me a hint?"

"I would, but——" A knock on the door interrupted her explanation. "Excuse me. I have to get the door."

She ran to the door and opened it. Before she could say anything, Blake and Bliss surrounded her, hugging her tightly. Paityn wasn't overly emotional, but it felt good to hug her sisters, and she held on for longer than normal.

Finally pulling back, she smiled at the twins, noting the tears standing in Bliss' eyes. She brushed her cheek. "Don't cry."

"Please don't." Blake rolled her eyes. "It hasn't even been a month. Get it together."

"Leave me alone." Bliss elbowed Blake. "At least I don't have a black heart."

Paityn giggled. "Get in here." She pulled one of the rolling suitcases inside. "Are you hungry?"

Bliss patted her stomach. "You know it."

"I thought you weren't cooking," Blake said.

Paityn led them around the corner into the open living room area. "You know I wasn't going to let you come here without making your favorites."

"So, no Cuban food?" Blake asked. "Because I had my mouth set… Oooh wee. This place is gorgeous. Floor-to-ceiling windows, stunning artwork. And I love the color scheme. Everything just flows. Uncle Jax is doing big things."

Bishop glanced up from his phone and stood. "Hi."

Blake bit down on her thumbnail. "And apparently so are you," she muttered under her breath.

"Who is that, sissy?" Bliss whispered.

"And tell me he has a brother," Blake added.

Paityn rolled her eyes. "Shut up." She introduced them to Bishop. "He's an attorney at Pure Talent and he's helping me with my business."

"Oh, so you're helping her with the Big Ass D?" Blake asked, a wicked gleam in her eyes.

Bishop blinked. "Excuse me?"

Paityn glared at Blake. "He doesn't know about that yet," she said between clenched teeth. Leave it to her little sister to embarrass the hell out of her. "I'm sorry, Bishop. Don't mind her."

"Is that peach cobbler?" Blake asked.

"Yes," Bliss answered from the kitchen. She lifted the top off the pan. "And there's greens. And it smells like pulled pork. Yum."

Paityn shrugged when Bishop met her eyes. "Sisters."

"Right," he said. "I should probably get going, let you visit with your sisters. We'll talk."

"I'll walk you out."

He waved her off. "You don't have to."

"I do." Paityn walked him to the door. "Thanks for stopping by. I'm looking forward to working with you." She finally reached out to shake his hand.

When their palms met, she couldn't help but notice how the contact flooded her with warmth, from the tips of her fingers to her shoulders and throughout her body.

"It's good to meet you, Paityn." His husky, low voice made her want to lean into him.

She didn't, though. Slipping her hand from his, she nodded. "Right."

"I'll talk to you soon."

She nodded again. Because apparently she couldn't form any words.

Once he was safely outside the door, she exhaled. If every interaction with him ended with a handshake that somehow felt more like a kiss or a tender caress against her bare skin... *I'm definitely in trouble.*

Also by Elle Wright

Contemporary Romance

Edge of Scandal Series

The Forbidden Man

His All Night

Her Kind of Man

All He Wants for Christmas

Once Upon a Series

Beyond Forever (Once Upon a Bridesmaid)

Beyond Ever After (Once Upon a Baby)

Jacksons of Ann Arbor

It's Always Been You

Wherever You Are

Because Of You

All For You

Wellspring Series

Touched By You

Enticed By You

Pleasured By You

Pure Talent Series

The Way You Tempt Me

The Way You Hold Me

The Way You Love Me

Distinguished Gentlemen Series

The Closing Bid

Women of Park Manor

Her Little Secret

Carnivale Chronicles

Irresistible Temptation

Historical Romance

DECADES: A Journey of African American Romance
Made To Hold You (The 80s)

Suspense/Thriller

Basement Level 5: Never Scared

Connect with Elle!

Subscribe to my Newsletter
New Releases, Upcoming projects, and Freebies!

On Facebook,
Join my cocktail lounge for exclusive updates, drink recipes,
and lots of fun!
bit.ly/EllesCocktailLounge

Visit my website: www.ellewright.com

Email me at info@ellewright.com

facebook.com/ellewrightauthor
twitter.com/LWrightAuthor
instagram.com/lwrightauthor

Acknowledgments

First, I want to thank God for loving me.

To my husband and children, thank you for being my light, my everything. I love you so much.

To my sista friends, my lit sisters, you ROCK! You're amazing and I'm so blessed to know you!

A special shout-out to the amazing readers , bloggers, and awesome writers that I've met on this journey. Thanks for your support. I appreciate you!

About the Author

There was never a time when Elle Wright wasn't about to start a book, wasn't already deep in a book—or had just finished one. She grew up believing in the importance of reading, and became a lover of all things romance when her mother gave her her first romance novel. She lives in Michigan.

Connect with Elle!
www.ellewright.com
info@ellewright.com